Disclaimer

This book is a work of fiction. Names, characters, places, and incidents either are products of the author's imagination or are used fictitiously. Any resemblance to actual persons, living or dead, events, or locales is entirely coincidental.

All rights reserved. No part of this publication may be reproduced, distributed, or transmitted in any form or by any means, including photocopying, recording, or other electronic or mechanical methods, without the prior written permission of the author or the publisher, except in the case of brief quotations embodied in critical reviews and certain other noncommercial uses permitted by copyright law. For purchasing information or to obtain authorization for additional use of this material, please visit the appropriate publishing website or contact the author directly.

Copyright © [2024] by [Sarah K]

All rights reserved.

Table of Contents

Preface.................. 3

Chapter 1: First encounter (The Tarot's Whisper).......6

Chapter 2: Digital Heartbeats........22

Chapter 3: A Glance, A Thousand Words....................31

Chapter 4: The Illusion of Proximity....................40

Chapter 5: Obsession's Crescendo...46

Chapter 6: The Echoes of Limerence....................56

Chapter 7: The Unraveling....................66

Chapter 8: A Collision of Hearts........ 75

Chapter 9: Through the Looking Glass....................84

Chapter 10: Conversations with the Universe....................91

Epilogue: Love, Beyond the Screen...98

Preface

Hey there,

Before you dive into the world I have poured onto these pages, I want to share something with you. This novella? It's been a bit of a unique undertaking for me. I've always wanted to tell a story about the rollercoaster ride of love and the crazy journey of self-discovery. But, putting feelings into words, that's never been my strong suit. So, I decided to do something a little different—I teamed up with an AI to help me write this.

Think of it as having a ghostwriter but with a techy twist. The AI has been my sidekick, helping me translate my experiences into something that's artistic and speaks from the heart, especially from the view of someone who's been confused by love. We've all been there, right?

So, as you read, know that every word has come from the love, confusion, and joy of real human emotions, just with a little digital help. The journey you're about to jump into is one I've felt deeply, and now I'm stoked to share it with you, almost as if we're sitting down and chatting about it over coffee.

Let's begin.

Limerence:

Noun.

The state of being infatuated or obsessed with another person, typically experienced involuntarily, and characterized by an intense longing for reciprocation of one's feelings. It is marked by intrusive thoughts, fantasies, and intense emotional responses towards the object of affection.

Chapter 1: First encounter (The Tarot's Whisper)

I sat at my desk, a few minutes before I was supposed to go to bed. the soft glow of the lamp illuminating the scattered papers before me. My mind drifted back to those first three days, the moments that had seared themselves into my memory with a intensity I couldn't shake. I held my fuzzy pink pen and started writing:

Day one. I walked into the office, the familiar hum of activity enveloping me as I made my way to my desk. And there he was. Cody, the new intern, his head resting on his folded arms, lost in the depths of slumber. I approached him, my footsteps muffled by the plush carpet, and gently cleared my throat.

"Good morning," I said softly, not wanting to startle him. He stirred, lifting his head slowly, and my breath caught in my throat. Even with his face slightly puffy and tinged with the telltale signs of a restless night, he was striking. His chiseled jawline, the wayward strands of hair escaping from his perfectly tousled man bun, and the sharp lines of his office attire all conspired to leave me momentarily speechless.

"Morning," he mumbled, his voice thick with sleep. "Sorry, I didn't mean to doze off."

I waved off his apology, a smile tugging at the corners of my lips. "It's okay, it's your first day. Did you have trouble sleeping last night?"

He nodded, running a hand through his hair. "Yeah, just a bit of nerves, I guess."

I felt a surge of compassion for him, remembering my own first day jitters. "Don't worry, you'll do great. And if you need anything, I'm here to help. I'm Anna, by the way, your direct supervisor for training."

"Thanks, Anna. I'm Cody." He flashed me a grateful smile, and I felt my heart skip a beat.

As I walked away, I couldn't help but steal a glance back at him. Three words echoed in my mind: "Who is that?" I silently prayed for myself, knowing that I would be seeing him every day from now on. But even as I tried to push the thought aside, I couldn't deny the flicker of excitement that danced through my veins at the prospect.

Day two. I arrived at the office early, the morning sun casting a warm glow through the expansive windows. The company I worked for was a renowned tech firm, known for its cutting-edge innovations and dynamic work environment. I had graduated top of my class and had been promoted several times, eventually landing the position of head of the training department. It was a role I took great pride in, having helped countless trainees reach their potential and discover their unique strengths.

As I made my usual morning rounds, greeting the employees under my direct supervision, I tried to commit their names to memory. It was a challenge, as I had always struggled with remembering names, even though I never forgot a face. The sea of new faces and names swirled in my mind as I made my way through the office.

And then I saw him. He was sitting at his desk, his brow furrowed in concentration as he typed away on his keyboard. I approached him, a smile on my face.

"Good morning, Jake," I said, the wrong name slipping from my lips before I could catch it.

Cody looked up, a flicker of amusement in his eyes. "It's Cody, actually," he corrected me gently, his voice warm and friendly.

I felt my cheeks flush with embarrassment. "I'm so sorry, Cody. I'm usually better with names, I promise."

He laughed, a sound that sent a pleasant shiver down my spine. "No worries, Anna. I know you work with a lot of trainees and employees. It's totally normal to take some time to memorize names."

His understanding and kindness caught me off guard. Most people would have been annoyed or offended by my mistake, but Cody seemed to take it in stride. I found myself drawn to his easygoing nature, the way he could put me at ease with just a few words.

"Thank you for being so understanding," I said, my voice soft. "I'll make sure to remember your name from now on."

He grinned, his eyes crinkling at the corners. "I'll hold you to that."

As I walked away, I couldn't help but feel a sense of warmth spreading through my chest. Cody's presence had a way of brightening even the most mundane moments, and I found myself looking forward to our future interactions, however brief they might be.

As the day drew to a close, I found myself lingering at my office desk, my mind still preoccupied with thoughts of Cody. Despite the countless tasks and meetings that had filled my schedule, his presence had been a constant undercurrent, a gentle tug at the edges of my consciousness. Before clocking out, I decided to indulge my curiosity and search for his full name among the list of trainees for the first three months. I knew that he was placed in training within the marketing and communications technology department, a fact that I clung to like a lifeline as I scrolled through the seemingly endless rows of names and ID numbers.

My eyes scanned the spreadsheet, my heart racing with anticipation as I searched for the department name. And then, there it was, nestled between the lines of data: Marketing and Communications Technology. I felt a surge of excitement as I narrowed my focus, my gaze darting from name to name until it finally landed on the one I had been seeking.

Cody James Thompson. Born May 17th, 1999.

I stared at the screen, a sense of achievement washing over me as I committed his full name and birthdate to memory. It was a small victory, but one that filled me with a strange sense of satisfaction. Knowing his name felt like a tiny piece of him that I could carry with me, a secret that only I was privy to.

I leaned back in my chair, a smile playing at the corners of my lips as I savored the moment. The office around me had grown quiet, the usual bustle of activity replaced by a peaceful stillness. In that moment, it felt as though the world had narrowed down to just me and the glowing screen before me, Cody's name etched into the pixels like a promise.

Day three. The office buzzed with an unusual energy, a palpable excitement that seemed to permeate every corner of the building. It was the day of the welcome event for the new trainees, a small gesture of appreciation that Lila and I had been working tirelessly to organize. The training department had gone all out, arranging for a selection of delectable mocktails to be served during the extended break, a sweet treat to help the new hires feel at home.

As I made my way through the throng of people, I caught sight of Lila, her face lit up with a radiant smile. She waved me over, her eyes sparkling with the same enthusiasm that I felt coursing through my veins.

"Anna, can you believe this turnout?" she exclaimed, her voice barely audible over the lively chatter that filled the room. "Everyone seems to be having such a great time!"

I nodded, my own grin widening as I surveyed the scene before me. The trainees mingled with their colleagues, their laughter and animated conversations creating a warm, inviting atmosphere. It was moments like these that reminded me why I loved my job so much, the opportunity to make a difference in people's lives, no matter how small.

"We did a great job, Lila," I said, giving her a quick hug. "I couldn't have done it without you."

She returned the embrace, her smile never wavering. "Teamwork makes the dream work, right?"

As the event wound down and everyone began to trickle back to their respective offices, I felt a sense of contentment wash over me. It had been a success, a small victory in the grand scheme of things, but one that filled me with pride nonetheless.

I returned to my office, my mind already racing with ideas for the next event, when a soft knock at the door pulled me from my thoughts. I looked up to see Cody standing in the doorway, virgin mojito still in his hand, his expression a mix of nervousness and gratitude.

"Hey, Anna," he said, his voice soft. "I just wanted to thank you for organizing that event. It meant a lot to us newbies."

I felt my heart swell with emotion, touched by his sincere words. "It was my pleasure, Cody. I'm glad you enjoyed it."

What happened next caught me completely off guard. In a sudden, unexpected movement, Cody stepped forward and wrapped his arms around me, pulling me into a tight hug. For three seconds, I stood there, frozen, my mind reeling as I tried to process what was happening. And then, almost instinctively, I found myself returning the embrace, my own arms encircling his back, my hands patting him gently three times.

As quickly as it had begun, the hug ended, and Cody stepped back, a shy smile on his face. "Thanks again, Anna," he said, before turning and walking away, leaving me standing there, my heart racing and my mind spinning with a whirlwind of emotions.

I sat at my desk, my mind still reeling from the unexpected hug Cody had given me. The warmth of his embrace lingered on my skin, and I found myself struggling to focus on the work before me. I tried to finish up some tasks on my laptop, but my thoughts kept drifting back to that moment, replaying it over and over in my mind.

As I reached for my own drink, I noticed that Cody had left the rest of his mojito on my desk. I pulled it closer, the condensation cool against my fingertips, and I couldn't help but smile. The remnants of the drink seemed like a tangible reminder of our brief but meaningful interaction.

I couldn't help but wonder what the hug might have meant. Was it simply a friendly gesture of gratitude, or was there something more behind it? I knew that I shouldn't read too much into it, but I couldn't deny the way it made me feel. It was flattering, to say the least, to think that I had made such an impact on him.

Despite my better judgment, I found myself excusing his behavior, chalking it up to his youthful impulsiveness or perhaps his age. I didn't want to give him a hard time or make things awkward between us, so I decided not to mention it to him. It would be our little secret, a moment shared between us that no one else needed to know about.

With a sigh, I turned off my laptop and sat back in my chair, holding myself back from grinning like a fool. The memory of the hug played on a loop in my mind, and I knew that it would be a long time before I would be able to forget it.

As I gathered my things and prepared to leave for the day, I couldn't shake the feeling that something had shifted between Cody and me. It was a subtle change, but one that I knew would have a lasting impact on our relationship, both professionally and personally.

That evening, before drifting off to sleep, I found myself reaching for my phone, my curiosity getting the better of me. I couldn't resist the urge to look for Cody's social media profiles, to see if I could learn more about the man who had so quickly captured my attention.

I tried different possible handles, my heart racing with each failed attempt, until finally, there it was: "Cody.James99". I clicked on the profile, holding my breath as the page loaded, and I was thrilled to discover that his account was public.

I spent the next hour scrolling through his photos and posts, studying each image with a newfound appreciation. I was struck by his striking features, the sharp angles of his jawline and the intensity of his gaze. But what surprised me even more was the glimpse into his softer side.

There were videos of him playing the guitar, his fingers moving deftly over the strings as he lost himself in the music. And then there were the posts about his Muay Thai training, showcasing his dedication and discipline to the martial art.

I was elated to have found his online presence, to have this window into his life outside of the office. It felt like a small victory, a secret treasure that I could keep close to my heart.

As the days turned into weeks, my thoughts became increasingly consumed by you, Cody. Your presence lingered in my mind, occupying every waking moment and even invading my dreams. In the mornings, as I slowly emerged from the haze of sleep, your face was the first thing that came into focus. Those striking, gorgeous eyes that seemed to hold the secrets of the universe, and that stunning smile that could light up even the darkest of days. Throughout the day, I found myself lost in daydreams, imagining the two of us sharing happy moments together. I pictured us laughing at inside jokes, our hands brushing against each other's as we walked side by side. In those moments, the world around me faded away, and all that existed was the fantasy of you and me.

As night fell and I lay in bed, my thoughts drifted back to you once more. I recalled the details of your beautiful face, etching them into my memory like a precious work of art. Your cute nose, adorned with a smattering of freckles that I longed to trace with my fingertips. And those golden, curly locks that framed your face perfectly, begging to be touched and played with.

It was during one of these late-night reveries that I stumbled upon the word "limerence." As I delved deeper into its meaning, I realized that it perfectly encapsulated the intense, all-consuming feelings I had for you. The constant thoughts, the yearning for reciprocation, the involuntary nature of my emotions – it all made sense now.

Some people say that if a crush lasts for more than five months, then it's love. Well, here I am, five months and ten days later, and I'm starting to believe that what I felt for you from day one was indeed love. The kind of love that takes root in your heart and refuses to let go, the kind that makes you feel alive and terrified all at once.

The memory of that trainee welcome party is forever etched in my mind. It was a day filled with unexpected joy and a glimmer of hope that perhaps my feelings for you were not entirely one-sided.

The memory of you adding me on social media is another moment I cherish. You casually gave me your handle, and I pretended to be surprised, as if I hadn't already discovered it long ago. But now, it was official. We were connected in a new way, a virtual bond that held the promise of something more.

I am getting ahead of myself. I get so lost in the memories and details of our brief interactions and it's easy to get carried away reminiscing about the moments that made my heart flutter. But, let me take a step back and recount one of the first times Cody and I had an actual conversation in which I learned more about him as a person.

It happened on a seemingly ordinary day at work. I was walking down the hallway, my mind preoccupied with the tasks ahead, when I heard a familiar voice call out my name. I turned around and there he was, Cody, standing a few feet away with a warm smile on his face.

"Hey, Anna! How's it going?" he asked, his eyes twinkling with genuine interest.

I felt a surge of excitement coursing through my veins, but I managed to keep my composure. "I'm doing well, thanks for asking. How about you?"

We fell into step beside each other, our conversation flowing naturally as if we had known each other for years. Cody shared his passion for martial arts, his eyes lighting up as he described the discipline and dedication it required.

"It's not just about the physical aspect, you know?" he explained, his hands gesturing enthusiastically. "It's a mental and spiritual journey too. It helps me stay focused and centered."

I listened intently, fascinated by the depth of his commitment. As we talked, I noticed the slight weariness in his eyes, and I couldn't help but ask about it.

"You must train really hard," I remarked, my voice laced with admiration. "Is that why you sometimes doze off during the day?"

Cody chuckled, a hint of embarrassment crossing his features. "Yeah, I guess I push myself pretty hard. Sometimes I just need an unplanned rest to recharge."

I nodded in understanding, marveling at his dedication. In that moment, I didn't feel nervous by his presence. Instead, I felt an overwhelming sense of happiness and contentment.

Being face to face with Cody, learning more about him and his passions, filled me with a joy I couldn't quite describe.

As our conversation drew to a close and we parted ways, I couldn't wipe the smile off my face. The memory of that interaction would stay with me, a treasured moment in the tapestry of our growing connection.

I found myself consumed by thoughts of Cody, replaying our interactions in my mind, trying to decipher the hidden meanings behind his words and actions. That first hug had caught me off guard, leaving me both elated and perplexed. I couldn't help but wonder if there was more to it than just a friendly gesture.

One evening, as I mindlessly scrolled through social apps, a tarot reader's live stream caught my eye. Her name was Carmen, and she was offering readings to viewers.

Intrigued and desperate for answers, I decided to join in.

"Hi, Carmen," I typed in the chat, my heart pounding with anticipation. "I'm Anna. Can you do a compatibility reading for me and someone I'm interested in?"

Carmen's piercing gaze seemed to reach through the screen as she acknowledged my request. "Of course, Anna. What's the other person's name? And I need to know your horoscopes as well."

I hesitated for a moment before typing, I thought back to when I found Cody's info on the excel sheets. His birthdate was on May 17th making him a Taurus. "His name is Cody. Taurus."

Carmen shuffled her tarot cards, the sound of them cutting through the silence. She drew a few cards and laid them out on the table before her.

"Anna, I see that you are a few years older than Cody. Either that or you are somehow hold a higher ranking than him." she began, her voice laced with intrigue. My eyes widened in surprise. How could she have known that detail?

Carmen continued, "But age is just a number, and it seems that Cody is quite infatuated with you as well. He looks up to you, not just as a potential partner, but also as a role model in some way. Perhaps you two work together in some capacity?"

I leaned closer to the screen, hanging onto her every word. Carmen's insights were shockingly accurate, and I felt a glimmer of hope rising within me.

"Cody sees you as someone inspirational," Carmen revealed, a knowing smile playing on her lips. "The way he looks up to you is quite impressive. He sees you as a creative soul. You must really love your job and what you do. He sees as a butterfly that fills the space with positive energy."

My heart swelled with a mix of emotions - surprise, flattery, and a growing sense of connection to Cody. Carmen's words had confirmed what I had been secretly hoping for - that Cody's interest in me went beyond mere friendship.

As the reading came to an end, I thanked Carmen profusely, my mind reeling with the newfound knowledge. I couldn't help but feel a renewed sense of excitement and anticipation for what the future might hold.

Chapter 2: Digital heartbeat

I'll never forget that time when our eyes met in a crowded space. Not only was it crowded, but we were on different levels. I was on the ground, and you, Cody, were on the first level looking over the park in front of our office building. It was crazy to me how when I looked up you were already looking at ME. My God. It couldn't have been a coincidence. It just couldn't have been.

Questions raced through my mind. Why were you looking at me? Was it mere chance, or was there something more to it? I couldn't shake the feeling that this encounter held a deeper significance, a hidden meaning waiting to be uncovered.

The crowd continued to move around us, oblivious to the silent exchange that had just taken place. But for me, time seemed to stand still. I couldn't help but wonder what thoughts were running through your mind, Cody. Did you feel the same inexplicable pull that I did? Were you just as intrigued by this unexpected moment of connection?

As quickly as it had begun, the moment passed. The spell was broken, and the world came rushing back into focus. But the memory of that encounter lingered, forever imprinted in my mind. It was a curious encounter, one that left me with more questions than answers, but also with a sense of anticipation for what the future might hold.

It's these unplanned moments that I cherish. I find myself replaying these in my mind a lot. Here is another vivid memory of you. I had just returned from a two-week work trip, and there you were, Cody, descending the stairs like an angel from above. The sight of you in that angelic color I adore took my breath away. It was a moment of pure serendipity, a chance meeting that felt more magical than any of the planned encounters I had imagined in my head.

Without hesitation, I went in for a hug, my heart racing as I felt your warmth envelop me. Your words, "I missed you," echoed in my ears, and I couldn't help but think to myself, "My angel." The surprise of your second hug nearly made my heart burst from my chest. In that moment, nervousness was replaced by pure joy and contentment. Your scent, your presence, everything about you filled me with a sense of belonging.

Another time, you surprised me by coming into my office to say hello. Whether that was a planned visit or a coincidental passing, I couldn't be sure. But the moment I saw you, I couldn't resist the urge to hug you once more. The fresh floral perfume that lingered on your skin was unexpected for a man, but it was uniquely you, and I loved it all the more because of that.

As we stood there, I confessed my wish to see you more often, lamenting the hectic nature of work that kept us apart. "Is everything okay with you? All is good?" I asked, genuinely concerned about your well-being. Your response was lost to me as I focused on the feeling of your arms around me once more before you left.

And then, those words that made my heart skip a beat: "I just love you so much! I really love you." I wondered if you had heard about my inquiries about you earlier that day. Regardless, I couldn't help but respond with equal fervor, "I love you too. I love you more actually." Though I knew your love might have been platonic, I allowed myself to bask in the warmth of those words, cherishing each and every hug we shared, counting them like precious treasures in my heart. But here I go getting ahead of myself again retelling my favorite parts only.

One morning as I sat across from Cody in the small conference room, I couldn't help but notice the way the afternoon light filtered through the blinds, casting a soft glow on his features. His hair was pulled back into his signature man bun, and his eyes held a glimmer of anticipation as he waited for me to begin.

I shuffled the papers in front of me, trying to focus on the task at hand. "Cody, I wanted to discuss your performance as an intern over the past three months," I began, my voice steady despite the butterflies in my stomach. "Overall, you've done an excellent job. Your work ethic and dedication have not gone unnoticed." I continued:" your internship should span 2 years, it began in September of this year and we are currently nearing the three month mark. Considering everything I think you're on the right track.

A smile tugged at the corners of his lips, and he leaned forward slightly. "Thank you, Anna. I've been working hard to make a good impression."

I nodded, returning his smile. "It shows. Your contributions to the team have been invaluable." I glanced down at my notes, my brow furrowing slightly. "However, there have been a few instances where you've been absent without prior notice. Is everything alright?"

Cody's gaze dropped to his hands, and he fidgeted with his fingers. "I apologize for that. I had some personal matters to attend to, but I should have communicated better."

I felt a wave of concern wash over me. "Cody, if there's anything you need, please don't hesitate to reach out. I'm here to support you, not just as your boss, but as someone who cares about your well-being."

He looked up at me, his eyes softening. "I appreciate that, Anna. It means a lot to know that you have my back."

I reached out and placed my hand on his, giving it a gentle squeeze. "Of course. We're a team, and I want to see you succeed." I withdrew my hand, feeling a tingle where our skin had touched. "Now, let's discuss some strategies to help you improve your attendance and communication going forward."

As we delved into the details of his performance review, I couldn't help but steal glances at him, admiring the way his eyes lit up when he spoke about his passion for the work. The meeting flew by, and before I knew it, we were wrapping up.

"I'll be going on a short work trip for the next two weeks," I mentioned as we stood up from our seats. "But I want you to know that I'm just a phone call or email away if you need anything."

Cody nodded, his smile genuine. "Thank you, Anna. Best of luck on your trip!"

As we parted ways, I couldn't shake the feeling that something had shifted between us. The professional lines blurred, and I found myself longing for more moments like this, where I could see beyond the intern and catch a glimpse of the man beneath.

That evening, as I lay in bed, my mind kept replaying the moment my hand touched Cody's during our meeting. The guilt gnawed at me, a nagging reminder that I had crossed a line. As his boss and a seasoned professional, I should have known better than to blur the boundaries between us.

I tossed and turned, wrestling with my conscience. The warmth of his skin against mine, the way his eyes had softened when I offered my support—it all felt too intimate, too personal. I couldn't allow myself to be swept up in the tide of my own emotions.

With a heavy heart, I made a decision. I had to establish a clear line between us, to maintain the professionalism that our roles demanded. It was for the best, I told myself, even as a part of me yearned for the connection we had shared.

The next day, fate had other plans. As I walked through the office, lost in thought, I nearly collided with Cody. He beamed at me, his excitement palpable. "Anna! I was just coming to say hi."

I forced a smile, steeling myself against the warmth that threatened to melt my resolve. "Hello, Cody," I replied, my tone dry and distant. The words felt foreign on my tongue, a stark contrast to the ease with which we had conversed just a day before.

His brow furrowed, confusion clouding his features. "Is everything okay?"

I nodded curtly, avoiding his gaze. "Yes, everything's fine. If you'll excuse me, I have work to attend to." I brushed past him, my heart heavy with the weight of my decision.

That evening, as I sat alone in my apartment, the guilt resurfaced, mingling with doubt. Had I made the right choice by pushing Cody away? The memory of his crestfallen expression haunted me, and I couldn't shake the feeling that I had hurt him deeply.

I replayed our interaction over and over in my mind, analyzing every word, every gesture. The coldness in my voice, the way I had dismissed him so abruptly—it all felt wrong, like a betrayal of the trust we had built.

As the night wore on, I found myself questioning my own judgement. Was maintaining a strict professional distance truly the best course of action? Or was I letting my fear of vulnerability cloud my judgement, pushing away someone who genuinely cared for me?

I sighed, burying my face in my hands. The path forward was unclear, and I knew I would have to navigate this delicate situation with care. But for now, all I could do was sit with my guilt and doubt, hoping that in time, I would find the clarity I so desperately needed.

The month of October was a turning point for me. In an attempt to break free from the constant thoughts of you, Cody, I decided to join a gym and focus on my health. I threw myself into a rigorous workout routine, hitting every machine and pushing my body to its limits with high-intensity interval training (HIIT).

As I stepped onto the treadmill, the beat of Beyoncé's "Cuff It" from her Renaissance album pulsed through my earbuds. The music drowned out the world around me, but it couldn't silence the thoughts of you that consumed my mind. With each stride, each rep, your face flashed before my eyes, every detail etched into my memory.

Sweat dripped down my face as I pushed myself harder, trying to escape the relentless longing that gripped my heart. But no matter how much I tried to focus on the burn in my muscles or the rhythm of my breathing, you were always there, lingering in the back of my mind.

October brought an unexpected twist when I contracted Covid, forcing me to put my gym routine on hold. Now, as I contemplate returning to the gym, I feel my emotions reaching a crescendo once more. The absence of your presence in my life has left a void that I can't seem to fill. I've come to suspect that I may have ADHD, wondering if this obsessive fixation on you is somehow connected to it.

It's as if my mind latches onto you and refuses to let go, no matter how hard I try to redirect my thoughts.

In a desperate attempt to catch your attention, I find myself making choices based on what I think might impress you. Every outfit I buy, every nail design I choose, every hairstyle I try—it's all with the hope that you'll notice and appreciate the effort I put in. I can't help but wonder if you even see these little changes, if they register on your radar at all.

Without you, Cody, I feel lost and empty. The things that once brought me joy—my favorite meals, warm showers, long walks, and dressing up—have lost their luster. It's as if the colors have faded from my world, leaving everything dull and lifeless.

Chapter 3: A Glance, A Thousand Words

As I stepped into the office, the energy was palpable. The air buzzed with anticipation, and I couldn't help but feel a surge of excitement course through my veins. Today was the day we showcased our latest innovations to visitors from distant branches, and the entire building seemed to thrum with a sense of purpose.

I walked through the crowd, my heels clicking against the polished floor of the entrance hall. Colleagues hurried past, their faces alight with determination and pride. Snippets of conversation floated through the air, mingling with the distant hum of traffic from the streets below.

"Anna, there you are!" Lila, head of public relations department, waved me over to her desk. "I need you to double-check the presentation slides before the visitors arrive. We can't afford any mistakes today."

I nodded, my heart racing at the responsibility. "I'm on it, Lila. I'll make sure everything is perfect."

As I settled into my chair, my thoughts drifted to Cody. Would he be among the attendees today? The mere possibility sent a shiver down my spine. I hadn't seen him since our last encounter, when I had pushed him away in a misguided attempt to maintain a professional distance.

Regret gnawed at my insides as I recalled the hurt in his eyes. I had been so focused on protecting myself that I had failed to consider the impact of my actions on him. Now, with the prospect of seeing him again, I couldn't help but wonder if I had made a terrible mistake.

I shook my head, trying to clear my mind. I had a job to do, and I couldn't let my personal feelings interfere. With a deep breath, I immersed myself in the task at hand, reviewing each slide with meticulous attention to detail.

Time seemed to slip away as I worked, the minutes blurring together in a haze of concentration. It wasn't until a gentle tap on my shoulder jolted me back to reality that I realized how long I had been at it.

"They're here," Lila whispered, her eyes wide with a mix of nerves and excitement.

I swallowed hard, my heart pounding in my chest. This was it, the moment we had been preparing for. As I followed Lila towards the conference room, I couldn't shake the feeling that today would be a turning point, not just for our company, but for me as well.

I stood quietly in the office event square, my heart racing as I tried to maintain a composed demeanor. The air buzzed with anticipation as employees from various departments gathered, waiting for the visitors from the other branches to arrive. I scanned the crowd, my gaze drawn to the familiar figure standing just a few feet ahead of me—Cody.

His presence caught me off guard, and I found myself struggling to keep my eyes from lingering on his form. The way his curly golden curls hair fell softly against the nape of his neck, the confident set of his shoulders, his sharp and strong jawline—every detail seemed to captivate me. I couldn't help but wonder if he sensed my gaze, if he could feel the weight of my longing from across the room.

Suddenly, as if sensing my thoughts, I noticed with the corner of my eye Cody turn around and see me. But before I could lock my eyes with him he quickly he looked away, his gaze darting to the side as if caught off guard by my presence.

I felt a flicker of hope ignite in my chest. Could it be that he was as affected by me as I was by him? Was it possible that beneath his calm exterior, he too was grappling with the same intense emotions that consumed me?

We escorted the visitors to the conference room to start the presentation. and as the event continued, I found myself stealing glances at Cody, trying to decipher the meaning behind his actions. The way he shifted his weight from foot to foot, the way his fingers drummed against his thigh—every movement seemed to hold a secret message, a hidden clue to his true feelings.

But even as I searched for signs of his reciprocation, doubt crept in, whispering that I was merely projecting my desires onto him. The fear of rejection, of discovering that my feelings were one-sided, gnawed at the edges of my mind, threatening to unravel the fragile hope I clung to.

After the presentation was over and all the speakers left I stood by the door, my mind still reeling from the earlier encounter with Cody, I found myself engaged in a casual conversation with a coworker. We exchanged pleasantries, checking in on each other's well-being, but my attention was divided. From the corner of my eye, I couldn't help but notice Cody in the background, chatting with another colleague.

Suddenly, as my coworker bid me farewell and walked away, I saw Cody turn and make his way towards me. His walk was slightly off, a subtle limp in his step that caught my attention. Concern washed over me as he approached, and I couldn't help but ask, "Are you okay?"

Cody's face softened, a flicker of vulnerability crossing his features. "Oh, I just have some lower back pain from the other day when we were moving furniture."

I nodded, recalling the previous morning when I had noticed his discomfort. "Yeah, I noticed yesterday morning you were standing weird. You looked like you were in some pain."

A mischievous glint danced in Cody's eyes as he leaned in slightly, his voice lowering to a conspiratorial whisper. "Yes, keep your focus on me. I like that." With those words, he turned and walked away smoothly, leaving me stunned and flustered.

I couldn't help but feel a mix of confusion and intrigue. What was he trying to do? The sudden shift in his demeanor, from the coldness of the previous days to this flirtatious banter, left me reeling. I had always been observant, noticing the little things about him, like his habit of quickly glancing at his phone notifications during meetings when we weren't supposed to. But this? This was something entirely different.

As I watched him disappear down the hallway, I couldn't shake the feeling that something had changed between us. The air crackled with a new energy, a tension that both thrilled and terrified me. I found myself wondering what lay beneath the surface of his words, what hidden meanings and intentions he might be concealing.

I found myself questioning every interaction, every fleeting moment we shared. Were you experiencing the same overwhelming feelings as I was? Did you find yourself constantly thinking about me, seeking out my presence even in the most unlikely places?

The thought of you being limerent too sent a shiver down my spine. The idea that you might be planning what to say, hoping to bump into me, cherishing the gifts I gave you—it was both exhilarating and terrifying.

I couldn't help but chuckle as I recalled the moment with the nurse assistant. The way you had stepped in, your voice firm yet gentle, telling her not to be too harsh with me. It was a small gesture, but it spoke volumes about your care and concern for me.

And then there was the moment you handed me the meeting minutes along with a small piece of candy. Your fingers brushed against mine, lingering for just a second longer than necessary. I could feel the warmth of your touch, the sincerity in your eyes as you said, "Just for you." as you handed me the candy. It was a simple act, but it felt like a declaration of something deeper, something unspoken.

But amidst the excitement and the butterflies, there was also a sense of unease. Your words from earlier echoed in my mind: "Keep your focus on me. I like that." It was a bold statement, one that left me both flattered and unsettled. What were you trying to do? Were you testing the boundaries of our relationship, pushing to see how far you could go?

I found myself making excuses for your behavior, chalking it up to your youth and inexperience. In a way, I saw a reflection of my younger self in you—the impulsiveness, the desire to be noticed, the need for validation.

As the song "Remember the First Time" by Destiny's Child played in the background, I couldn't help but wonder if this was just the beginning of something new, something unexpected. The lyrics seemed to mirror my own thoughts, the uncertainty and the excitement of falling for someone who might just feel the same way.

I found myself sitting in the small conference room, my heart racing with anticipation as I waited for Cody's presentation to begin. It was one of the many items on the internship checklist, but for me, it held a special significance. It was a chance to see him in his element, to witness the charisma and confidence that had captivated me from the very first moment.

As Cody took the stage, I couldn't help but be mesmerized by his presence. His golden curls were pulled back into his signature bun, a style that accentuated his chiseled features and sharp jawline. His voice filled the room, commanding attention with every word he spoke.

Throughout the presentation, I found myself hanging onto his every word, my eyes locked on his face. The way he moved, the way he gestured with his hands—every action seemed to be imbued with a natural grace and poise.

When the presentation ended, I lingered in the room, hoping for a chance to speak with him one-on-one. As the other attendees filed out, Cody approached me, a warm smile on his face.

"Anna, thank you for coming," he said, his voice soft and sincere. "I really appreciate your support."

I couldn't help but return his smile, my cheeks flushing with a mixture of nerves and excitement. "Of course, Cody. Your presentation was incredible. Your charisma and confidence really shone through."

Cody ducked his head, a hint of shyness creeping into his demeanor. "Thank you, that means a lot coming from you."

We fell into easy conversation, discussing his hobbies and interests outside of work. I was curious to know how he had developed such strong public speaking skills and charisma.

"My mother has always made it a point to teach me about different cultures," Cody explained, his eyes lighting up with passion. "She's from Thailand, and she's instilled in me a love for travel and exploring new places."

As he spoke about his heritage and his life experiences, I found myself drawn in even further. There was a depth to him that I had never seen before, a richness of character that went beyond his striking appearance.

As our conversation continued, I found myself getting lost in his words, in the way his eyes sparkled with enthusiasm. It was a side of Cody that I had never seen before, and I couldn't help but feel a sense of privilege at being allowed a glimpse into his world.

Chapter 4: The illusion of proximity

I walked into the office, my eyes instinctively scanning the familiar surroundings for a glimpse of Cody. It had become a ritual, a secret game I played with myself every morning. As I made my way through the bustling corridors, I caught sight of him near the water cooler, his golden curls gleaming under the morning sun rays.

I paused for a moment, taking in the details of his appearance. Today, he wore a fitted navy blue shirt that accentuated his broad shoulders and a pair of dark pants that hugged his lean frame. His hair was pulled back into his signature man bun, a few stray curls escaping to frame his face.

As I continued my journey to my desk, I couldn't help but plan our potential encounters. I knew Cody often frequented the break room around mid-morning, so I made a mental note to time my coffee break accordingly. The thought of casually bumping into him, exchanging a few words and a warm smile, sent a flutter through my chest.

But life has a way of throwing curveballs, and as I turned the corner, I found myself face to face with Cody. He was walking towards me, his eyes locked on his phone, unaware of my presence. I felt a sudden surge of nerves, my heart racing as I tried to compose myself.

Just as he looked up, our eyes met, and a smile spread across his face. "Good morning, Anna," he said, his voice warm and inviting.

I returned his smile, hoping my nerves didn't show. "Morning, Cody. How's your day going so far?"

He shrugged, a playful glint in his eyes. "Oh, you know, the usual. Meetings, emails, and trying to keep the coffee machine from staging a rebellion."

I laughed, the tension in my body easing with his humor. "Well, if you need backup, just give me a signal. I've got your back."

Cody grinned, his dimples appearing in his cheeks. "I'll keep that in mind. Thanks, Anna."

As we parted ways, I couldn't help but feel a sense of elation. These small moments, these brief interactions, were the highlights of my day. They fueled my imagination, my hopes, and my dreams of what could be.

I couldn't help but feel a wave of emotions wash over me as I sat on my bed that night, my mind consumed by thoughts of Cody. He had come into my life like a whirlwind, sweeping me off my feet and reigniting a spark within me that I had long forgotten. The mere thought of him brought a smile to my face, and I found myself eagerly anticipating every interaction we shared.

I reached for my phone, my fingers itching to check my social media feeds for any updates from him. It had become a ritual, a way to feel connected to him even when we were apart. Seeing his posts, his pictures, his words—it all filled me with a sense of joy and anticipation.

But as the hours ticked by, the emptiness crept in. It was 9 pm, and the restlessness that had been building throughout the day reached a crescendo. I paced around my room, my mind racing with thoughts of Cody and the uncertainty of our relationship.

I had tried to rationalize my feelings, to convince myself that we were from different worlds, that this infatuation was nothing more than a fleeting fantasy. But no matter how hard I tried, I couldn't shake the hold he had on me. The more I fought against it, the deeper I seemed to fall.

The unfinished tasks of the day mocked me, reminding me of how consumed I had become by my own emotions. The laundry lay untouched, the errands left undone. I felt trapped in a cycle of longing and frustration, unable to break free from the grip of my own heart.

I collapsed onto my bed, burying my face in my hands. The tears came unbidden, a release of the pent-up emotions that had been building inside me. I knew I needed help, a way to navigate the tumultuous waters of my own feelings. But where could I turn? Who could understand the depth of my infatuation, the intensity of my longing?

As I lay there, my thoughts drifted to Cody once more. I couldn't help but wonder if he felt the same way, if he too was consumed by thoughts of me. The possibility both thrilled and terrified me, a double-edged sword that cut deep into my soul.

As I lay there, consumed by my thoughts of Cody, I found myself reaching for my phone once more. My fingers moved on their own accord, opening one of those social apps, seeking solace in the digital world. The algorithm seemed to sense my yearning, and the first video that appeared on my "For you" homepage was a collective reading, brimming with hope.

The tarot reader's words echoed in my mind, "The person you are thinking about is thinking about you too, but is afraid to confess because of some limitations. You must be patient and be confident that your lover will find you." My heart skipped a beat, a flicker of possibility igniting within me.

And then, as if the universe itself had conspired to send me a message, a tarot reading appeared on my screen, proclaiming, "This horoscope is madly in love with you. Taurus."

My breath caught in my throat, and I felt a shiver run down my spine. Cody's birthday was in May, making him a Taurus. Could it be a sign? A cosmic confirmation of the connection I felt between us?

I replayed the video, hanging onto every word, every gesture of the tarot reader. The synchronicity was uncanny, and I couldn't help but feel a glimmer of hope reigniting within me.

As I scrolled further, another video caught my attention. It mentioned limerence and ADHD in the same breath, a combination that struck a chord within me. I had always been an overachiever, driven by a relentless pursuit of excellence. The thought of being ADHD made me uncomfortable, a label I wasn't quite ready to embrace.

The next morning, I stepped foot into the office, ready to embark on my daily "Cody" routine. As I descended the stairs from the third floor, I couldn't resist the urge to peek out the window. There he was, arriving at the office building, his golden curls bouncing off his shoulders as he paced quickly, his black laptop bag slung over his shoulder. I quickened my steps, hoping to catch him at the bottom of the stairs. My heart raced with anticipation, the possibility of a chance encounter fueling my every move. But as I reached the end of the stairs, I realized he had already passed me by, heading straight to his office.

Disappointment washed over me, but I pushed it aside, focusing on the tasks at hand. I picked up what I needed from the office downstairs and made my way back up. As I reached the third floor, I found myself drawn to the window once more.

There he stood, outside with a few coworkers. I was three stories high, but the distance seemed to vanish as our eyes met. Lila, stood next to me, but my attention was solely on Cody. I waved to the others who recognized me from afar, but my gaze remained fixed on him.

He was already looking at me, his sweet smile radiating warmth. In that moment, it felt as though the world had faded away, leaving only the two of us. I gave him a slow blink and a big smile, a silent exchange that spoke volumes. As I looked away, I found myself trying to read his eyes, to decipher the unspoken emotions that lingered between us.

Chapter 5: Obsession's Crescendo

The crisp January air nipped at my skin as I made my way to the company event square. The annual team-building event and exhibition was in full swing, and the excitement was palpable. I spotted familiar faces from various departments, trainees, and even members from other branches. I stepped into the venue, marveling at the transformation that had taken place. The open concept design allowed for a seamless flow of energy, with various stations and displays strategically placed throughout the space. The sleek, modern aesthetic was a testament to the company's commitment to innovation and progress.

As I made my way through the crowd, I couldn't help but feel a sense of pride swelling within me. The event had come together beautifully, surpassing any of our previous gatherings. The integration of cutting-edge technology was evident in every corner, from the interactive displays to the immersive virtual reality experiences.

I paused for a moment, taking in the buzz of excitement that filled the air. Colleagues and industry professionals mingled; their faces lit up with genuine enthusiasm. The energy was palpable, a testament to the hard work and dedication that had gone into making this event a reality.

As I watched the attendees engage with the various exhibits, I couldn't help but reflect on my own journey with the company. Over the years, it had become more than just a place of work; it had become a second home. The support and camaraderie I had found here had been instrumental in my personal and professional growth.

I scanned the crowd, my eyes searching for one person in particular—Cody. Ever since our last encounter, I couldn't shake the feeling that there was a special connection between us.

I spotted him near the entrance, his golden curls catching the sunlight. I took a deep breath and approached him, a smile playing on my lips.

"Hey, Cody!" I greeted him warmly. "Welcome to the event. Have you had a chance to look around yet?"

He turned to face me, his eyes lighting up with recognition. "Anna, hey! No, I just got here. This place looks amazing!"

"Let me give you a quick tour," I offered, gesturing for him to follow me.

As we walked through the event square, I pointed out the various activities and booths set up for the day. We passed by the workshop zones, where experts were leading interactive sessions on emerging technologies and soft skills for the tech industry.

"Over there, we have the networking hubs," I explained, pointing to the curated spots with comfortable seating arrangements. "It's a great opportunity for interns like you to mingle with senior staff and exchange ideas."

Cody nodded, taking it all in. "This is incredible, Anna. I had no idea the company put so much effort into these events."

We continued our tour, stopping by the tech showcases and wellness corners. As we walked, our conversation flowed effortlessly, and I found myself drawn to his easygoing demeanor and genuine curiosity.

As we approached the innovation pitches platform, I noticed a group of employees gathered around a display of musical instruments. My heart skipped a beat when I saw a pair of guitars among them.

"Hey, Cody," I said, nudging him gently. "Do you play any instruments?"

His eyes widened with surprise. "Actually, yeah. I play the guitar. Do you?"

I couldn't help but grin. "I do! I've been playing since I was a teenager."

Cody's face lit up with excitement. "No way! We should jam together sometime."

In that moment, I felt a spark of connection, a shared passion that bridged the gap between our different roles in the company. We spent the next few minutes discussing our favorite songs and artists, our laughter mingling with the chatter of the event.

Somehow, as if drawn by an invisible force, we found ourselves sitting together, strumming different songs and taking turns singing alone. My fingers danced across the strings, muscle memory guiding me through the chords of my favorite song since I had known Cody: "Perfect" by Ed Sheeran.

The lyrics flowed from my lips, each word a testament to how I saw him. Perfect and sweet. As I sang, I poured my heart into every note, hoping he would understand the depth of my feelings.

Towards the end of the song, I caught Cody leaning towards one if his colleagues, whispering something. My heart raced as I watched her respond, wondering if he was asking about the song. A part of me hoped he would realize the significance of the lyrics, the way they encapsulated my perception of him.

As the final chords faded away, I felt a wave of nervousness wash over me. Performing in front of others had always been a challenge, but the moment I finished, the crowd erupted in cheers. Applause and words of encouragement filled the air, and I couldn't help but smile, basking in the warmth of their support.

Cody's eyes met mine, and for a brief moment, it felt as though we were the only two people in the world. His smile, so genuine and sweet, sent a flutter through my heart. I wondered if he could see the love that radiated from my eyes, the unspoken emotions that danced between us.

As the event continued, I gravitated towards Cody, our conversations flowing effortlessly. We laughed and joked, our shared love for music creating a bond that felt unbreakable. In those moments, I allowed myself to hope, to dream of a future where my feelings were reciprocated, where we could create a melody all our own.

As everything wound down at the end of the evening, Cody and I found ourselves sitting side by side, the conversation flowed effortlessly, as if we had known each other for years.

"I had no idea you played guitar so well," Cody said, his eyes sparkling with admiration. "How long have you been playing?"

I felt a blush creep onto my cheeks. "Since I was a teenager. Music has always been my escape, my way of expressing myself when words fail."

Cody nodded, a knowing smile on his lips. "I feel the same way. There's something magical about pouring your heart out through a song, isn't there?"

"Absolutely," I agreed, my heart swelling with the connection we shared. "Have you ever performed on stage before?"

His face lit up. "Yeah, a few times. Mostly at open mic nights and small gigs. It's nerve-wracking, but the rush of adrenaline is incredible."

I couldn't help but grin. "I know exactly what you mean. I remember my first time on stage, my hands shaking so badly I thought I'd drop my guitar. But the moment I started singing, everything else faded away."

Cody leaned in closer, his voice filled with excitement. "That's the best feeling, isn't it? When you're up there, lost in the music, and the audience is right there with you."

We traded stories of our performances, the highs and the lows, the moments that made our hearts soar. I found myself hanging onto his every word, captivated by the passion that radiated from him.

"We should jam together sometime," Cody suggested, his eyes locked on mine. "I bet our voices would blend perfectly."

My heart skipped a beat at the thought of singing with him, our harmonies intertwining. "I'd love that," I managed to say, my voice barely above a whisper.

As the conversation continued, I couldn't help but marvel at the serendipity of it all. To find someone who understood the power of music, who shared the same love for performing, felt like a gift from the universe. In that moment, sitting beside Cody, I felt a connection that went beyond mere infatuation. It was a bond forged through shared passions, a understanding that transcended words.

I woke up, my heart already racing with thoughts of Cody. It had become a familiar routine, reaching for my phone and checking his social media before even getting out of bed. As I scrolled through my feed, I froze, my breath catching in my throat.

There, in a series of stunning self-portraits, was Cody. Each image was more breathtaking than the last, capturing his beauty in a way that left me speechless. The way the light danced across his features, the intensity of his gaze, the slight curve of his lips—it was as if he had been crafted by the hands of a master artist.

I found myself lost in the depths of his eyes, wondering what secrets they held. Did they hide the same longing that consumed my heart? Or was I merely projecting my own desires onto him, seeing what I desperately wanted to believe?

The weight of my emotions crashed over me, a tidal wave of fear and uncertainty. I knew I couldn't confess my feelings, not now, not while we both worked at the same company. The risk of rejection, the potential for professional consequences, it all loomed over me like a dark cloud.

Self-doubt crept in, whispering insidious thoughts. What if I had misread the signs? What if Cody saw me as nothing more than a colleague, a friend at best?

I scrolled through the portraits again, each one a testament to Cody's effortless charm. The way he carried himself, the confidence that radiated from every image, it was intoxicating. I found myself drawn to him like a moth to a flame, unable to resist the pull of his presence.

Yet, even as I drowned in my own emotions, I clung to the faint hope that someday, when the timing was right, I would find the courage to confess. Maybe when one of us left the company, or when Cody finished his training, I could finally pour my heart out to him. Until then, I would continue to wait, to watch for any sign that my feelings might be reciprocated.

Later that day I was in my office sitting at my office desk. The gentle knock on my office door pulled me from my thoughts. I looked up, my heart skipping a beat as Cody stepped inside, a familiar smile on his lips. In his hand, he held a glass, condensation beading on its surface.

"Hey, Anna," he said, his voice warm and inviting. "I thought you might like a little pick-me-up."

As he approached my desk, I realized what he was holding: a virgin mojito, the very same drink he had brought me during our first encounter. The sight of it sent a rush of memories flooding through my mind—the laughter we had shared, the spark of connection that had ignited between us.

I accepted the glass, my fingers brushing against his for the briefest of moments. The cool, refreshing scent of mint and lime wafted up to me, and I couldn't help but smile.

"Thank you, Cody," I said, my voice soft. "I love mojitos!"

He grinned, leaning against the edge of my desk. "I thought you might like it."

I nodded, taking a sip of the mojito. The flavors danced on my tongue, transporting me back to that first shared moment. Cody's eyes sparkled with mischief. "I've been meaning to ask you something."

I raised an eyebrow, curiosity piqued. "Oh? What's that?"

He gestured towards my hands, his gaze lingering on my fingers. "How do you manage to play guitar so beautifully while keeping your nails looking so perfect? It's like magic."

A giggle escaped my lips, and I felt a blush creeping onto my cheeks. "It's not magic, I assure you. Just a lot of practice and a good manicurist."

We fell into an easy conversation about music, trading tips, and stories about our experiences. As we talked, I couldn't help but marvel at the way Cody made me feel—the warmth that spread through my chest, the flutter of butterflies in my stomach. before he left my office he tapped my elbow gently which sent a shiver down my spine and my legs felt numb again. Why does this keep happening to me? What is this effect he has on me?!

Chapter 6: The Echoes of Limerence

I walked through the office, as I navigated the maze of cubicles, my eyes couldn't help but seek him out, desperate for any sign of connection.

There he was, standing with two of his colleagues, their heads bent together in conversation. I caught Cody's gaze, and for a moment, time stood still. His eyes held mine, a flicker of something unreadable in their depths. Was it mere politeness, a social nicety ingrained in him? Or could it be a spark of the same longing that consumed my every waking thought?

I raised my hand in a tentative wave, a small gesture of acknowledgment. To my surprise, Cody mirrored the action, his lips curving into a faint smile. But it was what happened next that sent my mind reeling.

As I walked past their group, I felt the weight of their stares on my back. Cody and his colleagues had fallen silent, their conversation abruptly halted by my presence. The air grew thick with unspoken words, and I couldn't shake the feeling that I had been the subject of their discussion.

Questions raced through my mind as I continued down the hallway. What had they been saying about me? Did Cody share the same thoughts and feelings that haunted my every waking moment? Or was I simply a topic of idle gossip, a name whispered in passing?

I replayed the moment in my head, analyzing every detail. The way Cody's eyes had lingered on mine, the slight hesitation in his smile. Could it be a sign of something more, a hidden depth to our connection?

But even as hope fluttered in my chest, doubt crept in, its icy tendrils wrapping around my heart. Perhaps I was reading too much into a fleeting moment, yet again projecting my own desires onto a simple interaction.

Later that day Cody stopped by my office. He walked in and approached my desk. As He leaned against my desk, his eyes sparkled with excitement. "Hey, Anna, I've been meaning to tell you something."

My heart skipped a beat, curiosity piqued. "Oh? What's that?"

"I've been training in Muay Thai for a while now, and I just found out that I've been selected to compete in an international championship in Bangkok!"

I couldn't help but mirror his enthusiasm. "Wow, Cody, that's incredible! I had no idea you were into Muay Thai."

He grinned, his passion evident. "It's been a huge part of my life. The art of eight limbs, they call it. Punches, kicks, knees, and elbows—it's a beautiful and powerful martial art."

As he spoke, I could picture him in the ring, his movements precise and fluid, captivating the audience with his skill and charisma. "That sounds amazing. When is the championship?"

"It's in a couple of months. I'll be training hard until then, and I'll be away for a few weeks for the competition."

My heart sank at the thought of his extended absence. "Oh, I see. Well, I'm sure you'll do great. You have a natural talent for capturing people's attention."

Cody laughed, his eyes crinkling at the corners. "Thanks, Anna. That means a lot coming from you."

As we continued to chat, my mind wandered to the upcoming few days or even weeks without him. Would our connection fade while he was away? Would he forget about the moments we shared?

I made a mental note to keep a close eye on his social media, eager for any updates or glimpses into his journey. I knew I would be his biggest cheerleader from afar, silently rooting for his success.

As Cody eventually took his leave, I couldn't help but feel a mix of excitement and apprehension. The thought of him pursuing his passion was thrilling, but the idea of being apart from him left a bittersweet taste in my mouth. I glanced at the empty mojito glass on my desk, a reminder of the connection we shared.

The memory of that moment in the bathroom flooded back to me as I sat on the cold tiles, wrapped in a towel, my hair still damp from the shower. Tears streamed down my face, the ache in my heart was palpable, a dull throb that seemed to echo through my entire being.

Why couldn't I keep Cody off my mind? The question haunted me, taunting me with its unanswerable nature. I found myself lost in a sea of emotions, drowning in the depths of my own longing and confusion.

As I write this, a sense of déjà vu washes over me. It is as if I had experienced this moment before now, the act of writing about my feelings and wallowing in self-pity. The familiarity of it all only serves to intensify the pain, a cruel reminder of the cyclical nature of my infatuation.

Two days had passed since Cody shared the news of his Muay Thai championship, and I found myself constantly refreshing his social media, desperate for any updates. The silence was deafening, each passing moment filled with a mixture of anticipation and dread.

Finally, a notification popped up on my screen. Cody had posted a picture, followed by a short video. My heart raced as I clicked on the post, eager to see what he had shared. The caption read, "Grateful to my amazing friends." As I scrolled through the images, my eyes landed on a photo that made my stomach twist. Cody stood close to a female Muay Thai teammate, her arms wrapped around him in a tight hug. They looked so comfortable together, their smiles radiating warmth and familiarity.

I felt a sharp pang of jealousy course through my veins. The sight of Cody in another woman's embrace shattered the illusions I had carefully constructed in my mind. I had convinced myself that our connection was special, that the moments we shared held a deeper meaning. But now, seeing him so close to someone else, I couldn't help but feel deceived.

The video played automatically, and I watched as Cody and his friend laughed and joked together, their camaraderie evident in every frame. Each second felt like a knife twisting in my heart, a painful reminder of the reality I had been so desperate to ignore.

I closed the app, unable to bear the sight any longer. Tears welled up in my eyes as I sat in the silence of my room, the weight of my emotions crushing me. I had been so foolish, so naive to believe that Cody could ever reciprocate my feelings. I had built up this fantasy in my head, convinced myself that our connection was something more than just a friendly workplace relationship.

But now, the truth was staring me in the face, and I couldn't ignore it any longer. Cody had his own life, his own friends, and his own interests. I was just a colleague, a passing acquaintance in the grand scheme of things.

With a heavy heart, I made a decision. I had to let go of my hopes, my dreams of a future with Cody. It was time to abandon any illusions of reciprocation and face the harsh reality that my feelings were one-sided. The pain was overwhelming, but I knew I had to move on, no matter how much it hurt.

I couldn't help but count down the days until Cody's return from the Muay Thai championship. Two weeks had never felt so long, each day dragging on with an agonizing slowness. I tried to immerse myself in work, hoping to distract my mind from the constant thoughts of him, but it was a futile effort.

The social media posts only added fuel to the fire of my limerence. Every image, every update from Cody felt like a dagger to my heart. I couldn't escape the mix of longing and despair that consumed me.

On the 20th of March, I found myself walking to my car in the parking lot after a particularly draining workday. My mind was a jumble of emotions: hunger, exhaustion, stress, and an overwhelming sense of emptiness. I felt burned out, unable to muster the energy to care about anything.

But above all, I was still trapped in the clutches of limerence.

"What the fuck," I muttered to myself as I climbed into my car.

The drive home was a blur, my thoughts swirling around Cody and the void his absence had left in my life. The next morning, I woke up with a startling realization: it had been days since I'd seen him, and the ache of missing him was almost unbearable.

A few days later, I felt a glimmer of hope. Maybe my brain was finally starting to heal. Cody's coldness towards me when we are physically apart seemed to be helping me detach. I experienced a sense of freedom as if the war within myself was finally coming to an end.

But then I remembered how he never reached out to me on social media. He might watch my stories, but he never hit the like button. I couldn't help but wonder if he did it just to get rid of the notification.

Despite the momentary reprieve, I knew that if I caught even a glimpse of him when I saw him, all those emotions would come rushing back. I was tired, worn down by the constant battle against my own feelings.

"Dear diary," I wrote, "I'll definitely let you know."

I felt empty, drained by the relentless cycle of limerence and the toll it had taken on my heart and mind.

The next morning as I walked through the parking lot, my heart skipped a beat when I noticed Cody's car parked in its usual spot. A wave of emotions washed over me—excitement, nervousness, and a touch of dread. After weeks of his absence, I wasn't sure what to expect from our reunion.

I took a deep breath, trying to calm my racing thoughts. The anticipation was almost too much to bear. Would he be happy to see me? Would he even acknowledge my presence? The uncertainty gnawed at me, leaving me feeling vulnerable and exposed.

As I approached the entrance, I couldn't help but glance over my shoulder, half-expecting to see Cody walking towards me. But he was nowhere to be seen. I pushed open the door and stepped inside, my senses heightened, alert for any sign of him.

The familiar scent of coffee and the buzz of morning conversations filled the air. I made my way to my office, my eyes darting around the room, searching for that familiar face. With each passing moment, the knot in my stomach tightened, and I could feel my palms growing clammy.

I sat down at my desk, trying to focus on the tasks at hand. But my mind kept wandering, conjuring up scenarios of our inevitable encounter. Would it be awkward? Would the connection we once shared still be there? I couldn't help but wonder if his time away had changed things between us.

As the minutes ticked by, I found myself glancing at the clock more frequently. Each passing hour felt like an eternity, and the anticipation was slowly eating away at me. I tried to immerse myself in work, but my thoughts kept drifting back to Cody.

Suddenly, I heard a familiar laugh echoing from the hallway. My heart leaped into my throat, and I felt a rush of adrenaline course through my veins. I knew that laugh anywhere—it was Cody.

I looked up just in time to see him walking into the office, his eyes scanning the room. For a brief moment, our gazes locked, and time seemed to stand still. A flurry of emotions played across his face—surprise, recognition, and something else I couldn't quite decipher.

He smiled, and I felt a warmth spreading through my chest. But before I could react, he was surrounded by colleagues, eagerly welcoming him back and bombarding him with questions about his Muay Thai championship.

I watched from a distance, my heart aching with a mixture of longing and uncertainty. I wanted to approach him, to say something, anything. But the words seemed to stick in my throat, and I found myself rooted to the spot.

As the day wore on, I caught glimpses of Cody throughout the office, always surrounded by others, always just out of reach. When the moment finally arrived, it was nothing like I had imagined. Cody greeted me with a casual half a hug, his face devoid of any special emotion. The blankness of his expression felt like a punch to the gut.

I retreated to my office, my mind reeling from the unexpected encounter. I sat at my desk, staring into space, desperately trying to make sense of it all. The rational part of me attempted to find explanations, to justify his behavior and soothe my wounded heart.

Chapter 7: The Unraveling

it's late April; the beginning of Taurus season.

April and May brought a bittersweet ache, as Taurus season bloomed around me. I found myself missing Cody, his presence sneaking into my thoughts, sometimes less frequently, but with an intensity that left me yearning for his voice, his touch. Jealousy burned through me, a horrible feeling that consumed my being. I longed for him, the absence of his presence a gaping void in my heart.

In my dreams, I saw him, his golden hair shimmering, his skin inviting my touch. We basked in each other's company, a euphoric bliss enveloping us. His short, golden locks framed his face, his smile sweet and eyes lovely. I drank in every detail, committing them to memory.

But as I woke, reality crashed down upon me. It had been weeks since I'd seen him outside of social media, weeks since I'd been graced with his presence. I missed his face, his energy, the way he made me feel alive.

I wondered if my brain, craving the rush I once experienced in his presence, had conjured him in my dreams, a desperate attempt to relive the euphoria. Dopamine is a hell of a drug.

No message from you now, nothing. I miss you so much, Cody. Still, everything I do is for you. My biggest motivation for change has been you. What now? My heart hurts when I remember you. I pray to God because this has been a lot. I don't know what to do.

It's the way I feel about you that makes this different from any of my past love interests. It was so unexpected how I fell for you. And what's more unexpected is how you used to shower me with public displays of affection, especially during the earlier days. but it's as if you are toying with my emotions. Because I don't know if you know how I feel about you.

The first time you jumped to hug me, my whole existence was shaken from its core. Your bubbly personality and lovely being—I'll admit that I want it all for me, but that's just selfish. I'm still falling deeper and deeper. That first time you hugged me, it lasted three seconds for sure, but it made me fall for you hard! And I miss that so much.

I know you're not the type to keep contact through social media at all, but in person, every time you get a chance to engage with me, you do just that, and I love it. I love every moment we share together, every touch, every smile, every laugh. It's in those moments that I feel most alive, most connected to you.

When am I ever going to wake up from this delusion that has consumed my life and took over my thoughts. It's so difficult to have to go through this.

I'll never forget how you made me feel. When I saw you, I would be at my happiest. When we hugged, it was euphoric to the point my legs would go numb. I can only imagine what it would be like to love you entirely. I would feel like my life experience was complete. Meaning, if I were to die, then I'd have no regrets.

But here I am, trapped in this endless cycle of longing and despair. The memories of your touch, your smile, your presence—they haunt me, taunting me with the possibility of what could have been. I find myself lost in a sea of emotions.

The days dragged on, each one marked by Cody's noticeable absence. His once vibrant presence in my life had dimmed, leaving me grappling with a growing sense of unease. I couldn't shake the feeling that his distance was deliberate, a conscious choice to pull away from me.

Despite the doubts swirling in my mind, I found myself hesitating to act on my emotions. The fear of rejection, of exposing my vulnerability, held me back. But as the longing grew, I knew I needed guidance, someone to confide in.

I found myself standing outside Lila's office, my hand poised to knock. Taking a deep breath, I rapped my knuckles against the door, my heart pounding in my chest.

Lila greeted me with a warm smile, gesturing for me to come in. As I settled into the chair across from her, I fidgeted with my hands, unsure of how to begin.

"Lila, I... I need some advice," I started, my voice barely above a whisper. "I have... feelings for someone."

Lila leaned forward, her eyes widening with interest. "Oh, do tell!"

I felt my cheeks flush, embarrassment washing over me. "It's just... I don't know what to do. I'm not sure if he feels the same way, and I'm scared to act on it."

Lila's expression softened. "Anna, remember our high school days? You were so free-spirited, so open to new experiences. What happened to that girl?"

I sighed, my gaze dropping to my lap. "High school happened. The bullying, the constant torment... it changed me. But that's a conversation for another day."

Lila reached out, placing a comforting hand on my arm. "I'm so sorry, Anna. I had no idea you went through that."

I felt tears prickling at the corners of my eyes, the pain of those memories resurfacing. "It's not something I talk about often."

"Well, I'm here for you, whenever you need to talk," Lila said, her voice filled with genuine concern. "And as for your love interest, don't be afraid to take a chance. You deserve happiness, Anna."

I nodded, a small smile tugging at my lips. "Thank you, Lila. I really appreciate your support."

"Anytime," Lila grinned. "Now, let's plan a girls' night soon. We can dive deeper into this over some wine and laughter."

As I left Lila's office, I felt a glimmer of hope, a renewed sense of courage. Maybe, just maybe, I could find the strength to confront my feelings and take a leap of faith.

I arrived at Lila's place, the weight of my thoughts heavy on my shoulders. As I stepped inside, the warmth of her home enveloped me, a stark contrast to the chilly evening air.

"Anna, you made it!" Lila greeted me with a hug, her smile infectious. "I've got a special treat for you tonight."

She led me to the kitchen, where a array of ingredients lay scattered across the counter. "Mojitos! but with a twist.

We're spiking them with Patron Silver, in honor of your amazing presentation and event organization skills."

I couldn't help but chuckle. "Lila, that was weeks ago. You're just looking for an excuse to drink."

Lila grinned, her eyes twinkling with mischief. "Guilty as charged. But seriously, you deserve to celebrate. You knocked it out of the park."

As she muddled the mint leaves and lime, the refreshing scent filled the air. I watched as she poured the clear liquid into the glasses, the Patron Silver swirling with the mojito mixture.

"So," Lila began, handing me my drink, "tell me about this new infatuation of yours."

I took a sip, the cool liquid soothing my nerves. But instead of diving into the topic at hand, I found myself steering the conversation in a different direction.

"Actually, Lila, I wanted to talk to you about something from my childhood."

Lila raised an eyebrow, curiosity etched on her face. "Oh? What's on your mind?"

I took a deep breath, the memories flooding back. "When I was in elementary school, there was this bully. He stole my textbooks one day, and I had to deal with it all on my own. I didn't want to bother my parents with it."

Lila's brow furrowed, confusion evident in her expression. "I'm sorry you had to go through that, Anna. But how does this relate to your infatuation?"

I paused, realizing the tangent I had gone on. "I... I'm not sure. I guess I just needed to get that off my chest."

Lila reached out, placing a comforting hand on my arm. "Hey, I'm here to listen, no matter what. If you need to talk about your childhood, I'm all ears."

I nodded, grateful for her support. The conversation may have taken an unexpected turn, but I knew that Lila would always be there for me, ready to lend an ear and a shoulder to lean on.

I took a deep breath, the weight of my past pressing down on my chest. Lila's comforting presence gave me the courage to delve deeper into the memories I had long buried.

"There's more," I began, my voice trembling slightly. "When I was 11, I had a creepy neighbor who used to stalk me on my way home from school."

Lila's eyes widened, her hand tightening around mine. "Oh my god, Anna. That's terrifying."

I nodded, the images flashing through my mind. "One day, he approached me in his car, offering me a ride. But something felt off, Lila. It was like a gut instinct screaming at me to run."

I could still feel the panic that had gripped me that day, the way my heart had pounded in my chest as I saw him getting out of the car, reaching for my arm.

"I took off," I continued, my voice barely above a whisper. "I ran as fast as I could, not stopping until I reached home. I was so scared, Lila. But I couldn't tell anyone, not even my mom."

Lila's expression softened, her eyes filled with empathy. "I'm so sorry you had to go through that alone, Anna. No one should have to carry that burden, especially not at such a young age."

I felt tears welling up in my eyes, the weight of those memories finally finding release. "I tried to tell my mom once, but she brushed it off, telling me not to make a big deal out of it. So I kept it to myself, all these years."

Lila pulled me into a hug, her arms wrapping around me in a comforting embrace. "I had no idea, Anna. But I'm so glad you're opening up now. It's never too late to seek help, to start healing."

As we sat there, our mojitos forgotten on the table, I felt a glimmer of hope, a sense that maybe, just maybe, I could finally start to face the demons of my past.

"You know," Lila said softly, "therapy really helped me when I was going through a rough patch. Maybe it's something you could consider, Anna. A safe space to work through these traumas."

I nodded, the idea taking root in my mind. "I think you're right, Lila. It's time I start taking care of myself, to stop carrying these burdens alone."

Chapter 8: A collision of hearts

As I walked through the office corridors, my heart skipped a beat when I caught sight of Cody rounding the corner. Our paths crossed unexpectedly, and he greeted me with a warm smile that made my insides flutter.

"Hey, Anna! I haven't seen you around much lately," he said, his voice tinged with surprise.

I tried to keep my composure, fighting the urge to let my emotions show. "Oh, hey Cody! Yeah, I'm not your direct supervisor anymore. It's just a routine rotation, you know? Different heads of department take turns mentoring, but they all report back to me about trainee affairs."

Cody's expression shifted, a hint of disappointment in his eyes. "Ah, I see. That's a shame, though. I really enjoyed having you as my mentor."

His words sent a thrill through me, and I couldn't help but analyze every syllable, searching for hidden meanings. Did he miss our interactions as much as I did?

"But you know," he continued, his tone softening, "I love seeing you around the office from time to time. Your presence is reassuring to me, Anna. You're one of the best people I've had the honor of dealing with."

My heart soared at his compliment, and I struggled to maintain a neutral expression. "That's so kind of you to say,

Cody. I'm glad I can be a positive presence in your work life."

As we stood there, an idea sparked in my mind. Cody's birthday was coming up, and I saw it as an opportunity to deepen our connection. I couldn't resist the urge to drop a hint, to gauge his reaction.

"You know, Cody," I said casually, "you act like such a Taurus."

His eyes widened in surprise, and a grin spread across his face. "Wait, how did you know I'm a Taurus?"

I felt a blush creeping up my cheeks, realizing I had revealed more than I intended. "Oh, just a lucky guess, I suppose. When's your birthday, if you don't mind me asking?"

Cody chuckled, his eyes twinkling with amusement. "May 17th. But seriously, how did you know?"

I shrugged, trying to play it cool. "I must have overheard it somewhere. Or maybe it is my intuition."

As we parted ways, my mind was already racing with ideas. I knew I had to do something special for Cody's birthday, a gesture that would show him how much I cared. Perhaps a thoughtful card, hand-picked to reflect his interests and personality. It was a small step, but one that held the promise of something more.

As May 17th arrived, I found myself ritualistically stalking Cody's social media profiles that evening. My heart sank when I stumbled upon pictures of him celebrating his birthday with close friends and family. A twinge of disappointment washed over me as I realized he hadn't included me in his special day.

I abandoned any grand gesture ideas and settled for sending him a direct message instead. "Happy birthday, Cody!" I typed, my fingers hovering over the keyboard as I agonized over the perfect adjective to add. Should I keep it professional or venture into more endearing territory?

As I hit send, a wave of self-pity engulfed me. I had been so fixated on someone who clearly wasn't thinking about me in any romantic capacity. The realization stung, and I couldn't help but wonder if Cody had been toying with my emotions all along. Or maybe I was the one reading too much between the lines, projecting my own desires onto every interaction.

I made a decision to distance myself from Cody. There was no excuse to maintain contact when it seemed like there was nothing substantial between us. It was time to move on and stop clinging to false hopes.

Before drifting off to sleep that night, I turned to my music app for solace. However, the preset playlist was filled with songs that plunged me right back into the depths of my limerence. Each melody and lyric reminded me of Cody, reigniting the ache of missing him all over again. The music, meant to provide comfort, only amplified the longing I had tried so hard to suppress.

As I lay in bed, my eyes glued to my phone screen, I couldn't help but refresh my inbox every few seconds. The anticipation was killing me. I had sent Cody a birthday message last night, and now I was desperately waiting for his reply.

The morning light filtered through my curtains, and I realized I had spent the entire night tossing and turning, my mind consumed by thoughts of Cody. I grabbed my phone, my heart racing as I saw a new notification. It was a message from Cody.

My fingers trembled as I tapped on the notification, revealing his response. Before I even read the words, I took a screenshot of the message, wanting to savor this moment of acknowledgment from him. It felt like a small victory, a tangible proof that he had thought of me, even if just for a fleeting moment.

I read his message, my eyes devouring every word. It was a simple "Thank you, Anna! I appreciate the birthday wishes." But to me, it meant the world. I couldn't stop smiling, my heart swelling with joy.

As I navigated to my own profile, I noticed that Cody had viewed my story from last night. It wasn't anything special, just a random snapshot of my evening, but seeing his name light up the viewers' list made my heart skip a beat. I couldn't help but wonder if he had lingered on my story, if he had thought about me while watching it.

I replayed the story, trying to see it through his eyes. Did he notice the subtle hints of my feelings for him? Did he read between the lines of my seemingly mundane post? I couldn't be sure, but the mere possibility filled me with a giddy excitement.

I spent the next few minutes analyzing every detail of our brief interaction. The timing of his reply, the choice of words, the fact that he had viewed my story - I searched for hidden meanings, for any sign that he reciprocated my feelings.

As I finally dragged myself out of bed, I couldn't shake the grin from my face. Cody's message had injected a burst of happiness into my day, and I clung to that feeling, cherishing the small moments of connection we shared.

As I sat in Lila's living room, surrounded by a handful of friends, I couldn't help but feel a sense of loneliness creeping in. Despite the laughter and chatter filling the air, my thoughts kept drifting back to Cody. His presence had become a balm to my soul, easing the ache of isolation that had long been my companion.

m

Lila's voice pulled me back to the present. "Anna, you're looking amazing these days! Your hair, your style - it's like you're glowing from within."

I smiled, running my fingers through my hair self-consciously. It was true; I had been putting more effort into y appearance lately. I had started wearing my hair down more often, embracing its natural waves and shine. My makeup routine had evolved, too, with a newfound confidence in experimenting with bolder looks.

"Thanks, Lila," I replied, feeling a warmth spread through my chest. "I guess I've just been feeling good lately."

"It shows," Lila said, her eyes twinkling with a hint of mischief. "So, tell me, if you could get a tattoo of anything, what would it be?"

I paused for a moment, considering the question. My mind immediately flashed to the virgin mojitos Cody and I had shared, the memory of that moment still vivid in my mind.

A smile tugged at the corners of my lips as I answered, "I think I'd get a simplistic tattoo of a mojito."

Lila raised an eyebrow, curiosity evident in her expression. "A mojito? Why's that?"

I hesitated, not wanting to disclose the true meaning behind my choice. The mojito represented a cherished moment with Cody, a symbol of the connection we had shared. It was a secret I wanted to keep close to my heart, a reminder of the happiness he had brought into my life.

"Oh, you know," I said with a shrug, trying to play it off casually. "I just really like mojitos."

Lila nodded, seeming to accept my answer. She moved on to the next person, asking them about their hypothetical tattoo choices. As the conversation continued around me, I couldn't help but wonder if Cody had noticed the changes in me, too. I wished he could see the positive impact he had on my life, how his presence had ignited a spark within me, inspiring me to embrace my own beauty and confidence.

I sat in my room, my finger hovering over the button that would hide Cody from my story views. A wave of frustration washed over me as I realized that my recent posts had been nothing more than a desperate attempt to capture his attention. It was a bitter pill to swallow, acknowledging that my motives had been so heavily oriented around him.

With a heavy heart, I pressed the button, effectively shutting Cody out of my online world. The act felt like a small rebellion against my own obsession, a step towards reclaiming my independence.

But I didn't stop there. I went on a digital purge, deleting every trace of my infatuation. The screen captures, the recordings of personalized tarot readings, and any tagged posts related to romance and limerence - all of it had to go. Each deletion felt like a weight lifting off my shoulders, a shedding of the layers of obsession that had consumed me.

Determined to find a way out of this emotional maze, I turned to Google for guidance. I scoured articles and forums, seeking advice on how to cope with limerence. I jotted down the steps that resonated with me, hoping that they would provide a roadmap to freedom from my own thoughts.

The following days brought a new challenge as I was tasked with giving workshops in the conference room. I steeled myself, determined to maintain a professional demeanor despite the turmoil within me. As I stood before the audience, I deliberately avoided making eye contact with Cody, fearing that any connection would shatter my fragile composure.

But with each passing day, guilt began to gnaw at me. I couldn't help but wonder if Cody had noticed my avoidance, if he was interpreting my behavior as a personal slight. The thought of him feeling hurt or confused by my actions weighed heavily on my conscience.

As I lay in bed each night, my mind raced with possibilities. Did Cody sense the tension between us? Was he questioning my sudden change in demeanor? The uncertainty ate away at me, leaving me tossing and turning until the early hours of the morning.

I knew I couldn't continue this way forever. Sooner or later, I would have to confront my feelings head-on, to find a way to navigate this complicated web of emotions without sacrificing my own well-being or the respect I had for Cody.

Chapter 9: Through the Looking Glass

As I stepped out of the office, my mind still reeling from the decision to distance myself from Cody, a familiar hue caught my eye. There, parked just a few spaces away from my own car, was a vehicle that bore an uncanny resemblance to the warm sunset orange Lexus ES I drove. My heart skipped a beat as I approached, my curiosity piqued by the coincidence.

I circled the car, taking in its sleek lines and shiny exterior. It was a different model; a BMW Z4 but the color was so strikingly similar that it felt like a sign from the universe. I couldn't help but wonder if this was a subtle hint at Cody's reciprocation, a cosmic wink that perhaps our feelings were more aligned than I had previously thought.

Lost in my own musings, I nearly jumped out of my skin when the car suddenly let out a loud unlocking sound. I whirled around, my heart pounding in my chest, only to find myself face to face with none other than Cody himself.

He grinned at me, his eyes sparkling with their usual mischief. "Hey, Anna! Fancy seeing you here."

I swallowed hard, trying to regain my composure. "Cody, hi. I was just admiring your new car. It's a great color."

"Thanks!" he said, running his hand along the hood. "I saw it and just knew I had to have it. Reminds me of a sunset, you know?"

I nodded, my mind racing with the implications of his words. Did he choose this color because of me? Was it a subconscious decision, or a deliberate one?

"Well, I should get going," Cody said, breaking me out of my reverie. "Got a lot of errands to run. See you around, Anna!"

With a wave, he slid into the driver's seat and started the engine. I watched as he pulled out of the parking lot, the orange car disappearing into the distance.

As I stood there, my own car keys dangling from my fingers, I couldn't shake the feeling that this encounter was more than just a coincidence. The limerence that I had tried so hard to suppress came rushing back, flooding my senses with a heady mix of hope and longing.

I knew I had to be careful, to guard my heart against the possibility of disappointment. But in that moment, as I climbed into my own car and started the engine, I couldn't help but feel a flicker of optimism that maybe, just maybe, Cody and I were meant to be more than just colleagues.

That night, as I lay in bed, my mind wandered to the recent events that had transpired. I couldn't help but feel a pang of regret for deleting the tarot screen recordings. It was as if I had erased a part of my own history, a tangible reminder of the depths of my feelings for Cody. The shame washed over me, a bitter reminder of my inability to maintain my resolve in the face of my all-consuming limerence.

As the darkness enveloped me, I found myself lost in thoughts of Cody's eyes. Those mesmerizing pools of warmth and mystery that seemed to hold the secrets of the universe. I longed to lose myself in their depths, to hold his gaze and feel the connection that I knew existed between us. The mere thought of being close to him sent shivers down my spine, igniting a fire within me that threatened to consume me whole.

Sleep eventually claimed me, but even in my dreams, Cody's presence lingered. This was the second time he had appeared in my subconscious, a testament to the hold he had over my heart and mind. Yet, there was something peculiar about these dreams. Cody never spoke a word. The silence that surrounded us was deafening, a stark contrast to the vivid imagery that played out before me.

I found myself wondering what this absence of dialogue could mean. Was it a reflection of the unspoken bond between us? Or was it a manifestation of the distance that still separated us in the waking world? The questions swirled in my mind, adding to the sense of yearning that consumed me.

As I tossed and turned, I couldn't escape the reality of my situation. My feelings for Cody were like a raging storm, threatening to sweep me away at any moment. Yet, in the harsh light of day, I knew that I had to find a way to navigate this tempest. I had to find the strength to face my emotions head-on, to confront the truth of my limerence and the challenges that lay ahead.

But for now, in the stillness of the night, I allowed myself to be lost in the memory of Cody's eyes and the promise of what could be. Tomorrow would bring its own trials, but tonight, I surrendered to the depths of my longing, knowing that somehow, someway, I would find a way to bridge the gap between my dreams and my reality.

I sat in my office, the early morning light filtering through the blinds, casting a soft glow on the cluttered desk before me. My mind was a whirlwind of thoughts, all centered around one person: Cody.

I couldn't shake the feeling that there was something more to our connection, something that went beyond the realm of mere coincidence. Maybe we were connected somehow through family or common friends, I thought, my heart racing at the possibility.

I opened up my laptop, my fingers flying across the keyboard as I navigated to Cody's social media profiles. I scoured his friend list, clicking on each name and scanning their profiles for any hint of a shared connection.

Hours passed as I fell down the rabbit hole of internet stalking, my eyes straining from the glare of the screen. I visited the profiles of Cody's family members, his childhood friends, even his high school classmates. But no matter how deep I dug, I couldn't find a single clue that pointed to a shared history between us.

Frustration welled up inside me as I slammed the laptop shut, the sound echoing in the quiet of my office. I rubbed my temples, trying to ease the tension that had settled there. Was I going crazy? Was this obsession with Cody nothing more than a figment of my overactive imagination?

I glanced at the clock, realizing that I had spent far too much time lost in my own thoughts. I needed to get ready for work, to face the day ahead and try to push these delusions from my mind.

As the summer months of June and July rolled by, I found myself immersed in a journey of self-discovery and self-care. With Cody away for yet another championship and traveling the world, I had the space to focus on my own well-being, both mentally and physically.

I threw myself into a routine of healthy eating and regular exercise, determined to prioritize my own needs. The gym became my sanctuary, a place where I could clear my mind and push my body to its limits. I reveled in the feeling of sweat dripping down my face, the burn of my muscles as I pushed through each rep.

Yet, even as I dedicated myself to this path of self-improvement, I couldn't help but find myself drawn to Cody's social media updates. I found myself scrolling through his posts, drinking in every detail of his adventures and achievements. I never dared to leave a public comment, but I couldn't resist the urge to send him the occasional message, a small way of staying connected to him.

I noticed that Cody rarely, if ever, liked my own posts. But when he did hit like on one of my stories, I found myself obsessively taking screenshots, preserving each fleeting moment of acknowledgment.

One day, as I was working out at the gym, the familiar strains of Beyoncé's "Cuff It" filled the air. The summer heat and the rays of the late August sun suddenly transported me back to that fateful September day when I first met Cody.

The memories washed over me like a tidal wave, overwhelming in their intensity. I remembered the way my heart had raced at the sight of him, the way his presence had consumed my every thought. The limerence that had gripped me then returned with a vengeance, flooding my senses and leaving me breathless.

As I moved through my workout, lost in the haze of memories, I found myself replaying every detail of that first encounter. The way his eyes had sparkled when he laughed, the way his voice had sent shivers down my spine. I remembered the all-consuming nature of my attraction, the way my mind had been filled with nothing but thoughts of him.

Chapter 10: Conversations with the Universe – Healing tides

As the days turned into weeks, I found myself growing increasingly restless. Cody's absence from social media had become a glaring void, I refreshed his profile obsessively, my heart sinking with each passing day that brought no new updates.

The doubts began to creep in, insidious whispers that ate away at my already fragile sense of security. Had he blocked me? The thought was almost too painful to bear.

In a moment of desperation, I did something I never thought I would do. I created a fake account, a digital disguise that would allow me to stalk him undetected. My fingers trembled as I typed in a false name and uploaded a generic profile picture, my heart pounding with a mixture of excitement and shame.

For weeks, I lurked in the shadows of his online presence, but as the days stretched on, I realized that there was nothing new to discover. Cody simply wasn't posting it seems as if he had seemingly disappeared from the digital world.

During one my stalking sprees I noticed that one of my colleagues posted something. The realization hit me like a ton of bricks as I stared at the screenshot posted on my colleague's post. Cody had been posting all along, just not on the platforms I had been obsessively checking. The image of him laughing and enjoying himself at the club with our coworker sent a sharp pang through my heart. The screenshot had been taken from an account that cody uses to post on a different platform.

I felt utterly foolish, like I had been chasing a ghost. All my attempts to stay connected, to maintain some semblance of a bond with Cody, had been in vain. He had moved on, living his life and sharing it with others, while I remained trapped in the cycle of my own limerence.

The sessions with my therapist had shed light on the roots of my obsession—a complex interplay of ADHD, OCD, and the lingering scars of childhood trauma. I had begun to understand how these factors had contributed to my low self-esteem and the intensity of my feelings for Cody.

But understanding didn't make it any easier to let go. The tides of limerence still crashed over me, threatening to pull me under with each swell of emotion. It was a constant battle, a relentless current that I had to fight against every single day.

I closed the app, feeling a mixture of anger and despair. How could I have been so naive, so blinded by my own desires? I had created a fake account just to stalk him, only to discover that he had been living his life without me all along.

The realization stung, but it also brought a sense of clarity. I couldn't keep living like this, trapped in a cycle of obsession and self-doubt. I needed to find a way to break free, to reclaim my sense of self and build a life that wasn't defined by my feelings for someone who clearly didn't reciprocate them.

I took a deep breath, my fingers hovering over the delete button on the fake account. It was time to let go, to stop chasing shadows and start living in the light. I knew it wouldn't be easy, but I also knew that I had the strength within me to overcome this.

With a final, resolute click, I deleted the account and closed my laptop. It was time to face reality, to embrace the challenges ahead and find my way back to myself.

I couldn't resist the temptation to check the tarot readings one last time. As I scrolled through the app, a particular video caught my eye. The reader spoke about someone who looked up to you, someone who loved your body and the way you smelled. My mind instantly flashed back to the time when Cody greeted me with a hug, and I caught a whiff of his floral scent. It was intoxicating, and the memory alone was enough to send me spiraling back into the depths of limerence.

For a moment, I allowed myself to get lost in the fantasy, imagining what it would be like if Cody truly felt that way about me. The thought of him admiring my body and being drawn to my scent was both thrilling and terrifying. I could feel the familiar rush of emotions, the quickening of my heartbeat, and the flutter of butterflies in my stomach.

But then, as quickly as the fantasy had taken hold, I snapped back to reality. I knew I couldn't keep doing this to myself. I couldn't keep feeding the flames of my obsession, no matter how enticing the tarot readings might be. With a heavy heart, I unfollowed the account, determined to move forward and break free from the cycle of limerence.

"I've been feeling so desperate for reciprocation," I confessed, my voice trembling slightly as I sat across from my therapist. "It's like I'm constantly seeking validation, constantly hoping that Cody will finally acknowledge my feelings."

My therapist nodded, her eyes filled with understanding. "It sounds like the fear of missing out might be playing a role here, Anna. Your ADHD can amplify those feelings, making it even harder to manage your emotions."

I sighed, knowing she was right. "I've been trying to stay on top of my medication and CBT sessions, but it's still a struggle."

"That's a great step, Anna. Acknowledging your ADHD and finding healthy ways to manage it is crucial." She paused for a moment, seeming to consider her next words carefully. "I have a theory I'd like to share with you, if you're open to it."

I leaned forward, intrigued. "Of course, please go on."

"You've mentioned that you've had different objects of limerence throughout your life, fixating on them uncontrollably. But this time, you have the awareness to navigate your emotions in a way you haven't before." She looked at me intently. "Perhaps every time you fall into limerence, what you're really doing is admiring how skillful you are at dealing with them."

I furrowed my brow, trying to process her words. "What do you mean?"

"Anna, you're a very successful woman. You've reached incredible heights in your career, and you're admired by your peers and people in your field. You've achieved so much in every aspect of your life." She smiled softly. "But limerence is never really about the other person. It's more about you, Anna. It's about recognizing your own strengths and capabilities."

I interrupted, feeling a twinge of frustration. "But my personal life is a mess. How can that be about my strengths?"

"Because even in the midst of this struggle, you're still here. You're still fighting, still seeking help and working to understand yourself better. That takes immense strength and courage."

I felt a lump form in my throat, overwhelmed by her words. "Thank you," I managed to whisper. "I'm so grateful for your help. I'm determined to get my life better than ever."

I felt a sudden wave of gratitude wash over me. Despite the pain and the struggle, I realized that the universe was conspiring to heal me. Through confronting my trauma head-on and acknowledging how I had internalized it, life was giving me a chance to bring balance back into my existence.

I knew that nothing could be sustained without balance, and I had been teetering on the edge of chaos for far too long. It was time to embrace the awareness that had been granted to me, to use it as a tool for growth and transformation.

Epilogue – Love beyond the screen

Three years had passed since I opened my heart to the unexpected, to Cody, and most importantly, to myself. Standing at my favorite café, staring out at a city that once felt like a maze of lonesome digital screens, I now saw a canvas of genuine connections. I was no longer a spectator but a vibrant participant.

Cody played a role in my epiphany, a wandering muse who walked into my life and left footprints on my journey to healing. I took a sip of my coffee latte, savoring the warmth that spread through my body. It was a sensation that mirrored the contentment I felt in my heart. The past three years had been a transformative experience, a journey of self-discovery and growth that had led me to this very moment.

I thought back to the early days of my limerence, the all-consuming desire to be near Cody, to bask in his presence. It was a feeling that had consumed me, driving me to obsession and desperation. But through the guidance of my therapist and the support of those closest to me, I had learned to channel that energy into something more productive, more fulfilling.

As I watched the bustling city streets, I felt a sense of gratitude wash over me. I was grateful for the challenges I had faced, for the lessons I had learned, and for the person I had become. I was no longer the same Anna who had first laid eyes on Cody all those years ago. I was stronger, wiser, and more in tune with myself than ever before.

The tune from the street performer drifted through the air, a melody that once stirred a tempest within my heart. But now, it was simply a beautiful composition, no longer tethered to the depths of my soul. I smiled, acknowledging the growth and transformation I had undergone.

As I sat in the café, sipping my coffee and reflecting on my journey, I realized that my story wasn't just about falling in love with Cody. It was about falling in love with myself, embracing my vulnerabilities, and finding strength in authenticity. The digital accolades and curated personas that once consumed me had faded in significance, replaced by a wealth of self-acceptance and the love of those who truly mattered.

Beside my laptop lay a note, a habit I had picked up during therapy. The words "Live fully, love deeply, and let the universe do its work" stared back at me, a simple yet profound truth that had taken years to internalize. I smiled, acknowledging the wisdom in those words.

Life, I had learned, was an ever-evolving journey, much like technology. It wasn't meant to be scrolled through hastily, but rather experienced fully—one genuine, unfiltered moment at a time. I had once sought validation and fulfillment through the lens of others, but now I understood that the most profound romance was the one I had with myself.

As I savored the last sip of my coffee, I felt a sense of peace wash over me. The chapters of my life that had once been filled with doubt and longing had given way to a narrative of self-discovery and growth. I had learned to embrace the raw, unedited moments of life, finding beauty in the imperfections and strength in vulnerability.

Printed in Great Britain
by Amazon